S0-AQL-066

GOGO

THE FRENCH SEA GULL

GOGO

THE FRENCH SEA GULL

BY

LOUIS SLOBODKIN

THE MACMILLAN COMPANY NEW YORK

© Louis Slobodkin 1960

First Printing

The Macmillan Company, New York

Printed in the United States of America

Library of Congress catalog card number: 60–11819

Brett-Macmillan Ltd., Galt, Ontario

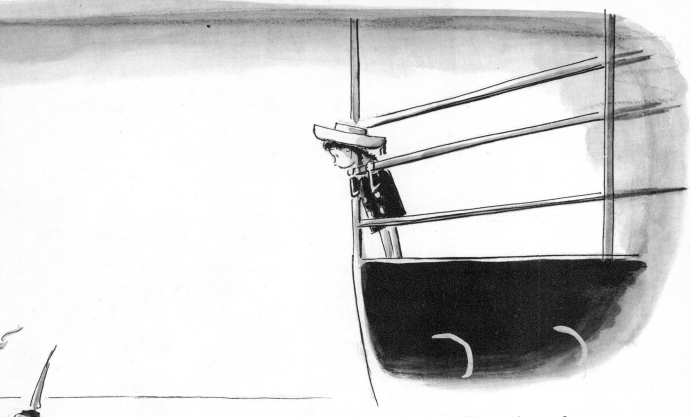

Gogo was a young French sea gull who looked like and acted like any other sea gull that lived along the coast of France . . . except for one very special thing.

Gogo was very fussy about his food. He liked good food . . . well cooked!

It was a little girl named Marianna who first found out about that one very special thing, and it was Marianna, too, who first called the young French sea gull Gogo.

Here is how it all happened.

Marianna and her mother were returning to America after visiting Marianna's grandparents in France.

Early in the afternoon they came aboard a big passenger ship named the *Queen of France*. While Marianna's mother unpacked their things, Marianna went out on deck to look over the rail at the busy harbor. Sea gulls were flying all over the place.

Some sea gulls followed the little fishing ships and ate the things the fishermen threw away as they cleaned the fish they had caught. Other sea gulls soared over the harbor and dove now and then to pick up some trash that floated on the muddy waters. And still other sea gulls stalked along the shore and pecked at unpleasant-looking objects washed up by the waves.

But there was one young sea gull who sat by himself on a pole down on the dock. He sat there watching the great crates of good food that were being loaded onto the *Queen of France*.

Marianna looked at that lonely young sea gull for a while and she worried about him.

"He should eat something," she said to herself. "He looks very thin."

She shouted softly down at the young sea gull.

"Hey you . . . sea gull! . . Go find something to eat . . . Please go, sea gull . . . Go . . Go . . Go."

The sea gull looked up at her and then turned his head again to look at the big crates of food.

"Go . . Go . . . Sea gull . . GoGo . !" shouted Marianna very loud.

"Is this the sea gull's name . . . GoGo?" asked someone standing at Marianna's side.

Marianna turned and looked up at a big red-faced man dressed all in white and with brass buttons.

"Oh, I just . . ." said Marianna, "I just called him to go . . . go and eat . . . He looks so thin. Are you the Captain of the ship?"

The big man laughed.

"No . . No, no . . . I am the Captain of the Kitchen," said the big man proudly. "I am the Chief Chef of the *Queen of France*. The greatest chef who sails the seas."

"O-h-h-!" said Marianna.

"Gogo is a fine name for a sea gull," said the Chief Chef. "You are very bright to think of that name."

"Thank you," said Marianna. "I shall call that sea gull Gogo from now on."

"Good," said the Chief Chef. Then he shouted down to the men on the dock, who had almost dropped a large crate marked GARLIC, "Be careful! . . Be careful! . . Garlic is very important in my cooking . . ."

Marianna went back to see if she could help her mother with the unpacking.

When the *Queen of France* started to leave the dock a little while later, Marianna, holding her mother's hand, came out on deck again. Everyone seemed very happy and excited. The people on the ship waved good-by to the people on the dock. And the people on the dock waved back.

Marianna looked for the thin sea gull she called Gogo. She wanted to wave good-by to him.

But Gogo was not sitting on the pole any longer. Marianna pulled her mother's hand.

"Mama, he's gone," said Marianna.

"Who's gone?" asked her mother.

"My sea gull friend," said Marianna.

"Really," said her mother. "But there are a lot of other sea gulls flying up over the ship . . . See them?"

Marianna looked up at the sea gulls whirling above the ship. Suddenly she shouted:

"There he is! Look, Mama . . . There's GOGO!"

"Gogo?" said her mother. "Who is Gogo?"

"Gogo is my sea gull friend," said Marianna. "See him, Mama? He's the thin sea gull leading all the others."

Her mother looked up . . . Then she nodded her head.

"Yes, I see him," she said. "Now let's go in and have our dinner."

Marianna waved at Gogo and went with her mother.

After the best dinner they had ever eaten (that's what Marianna's mother said), Marianna went out on deck again to see the sunset.

The big Chief Chef of the *Queen of France* was standing at the rail watching some men throw the leftovers into the ocean. A flock of sea gulls raced each other for the things that were thrown off the ship.

And the swiftest sea gull . . . the one who caught the best morsels of leftover food even before they hit the water . . . was GOGO!

"A very successful dinner," said the Chief Chef proudly to the men who were throwing away the leftovers. "There are very few leftovers. Our passengers know good food when it is served to them." The men nodded and kept on working.

"Gogo knows good food too," said Marianna.

The Chief Chef turned and looked down at her.

"That is Gogo," said Marianna, pointing to the sea gulls. "My friend Gogo . . . That skinny sea gull there . . . He knows good food too."

The Chief Chef watched Gogo dart like an arrow after the best leftover food.

"H-m-m . . . Yes, perhaps he does," he said slowly, "perhaps he does . . ."

From then on after every meal Marianna came out on deck and watched the sea gulls chase after the leftovers. She would stand alongside the Chief Chef at the rail. Sometimes she heard him mumble when there were too many leftovers thrown away, "H-mm . . . Yes . . . I thought there was too much salt on the buttered turnips."

Or he would say, "H-m-m . . . These passengers are stupid. They don't know how to eat good food . . . Look, they left the artichokes."

But Gogo liked everything the Chief Chef cooked. He did not mind a little too much salt and he just loved artichokes. He knew the Chief Chef of the *Queen of France* was the greatest chef who sailed the seas. And he proved that when the time came for the French sea gulls to leave the *Queen of France* and fly back to their native land.

Marianna found out (her mother told her) that sea gulls never follow a ship from France all the way across the Atlantic Ocean. They usually fly after the ship for about two days. Then they turn and follow some other ship back to France.

For a few days out in the middle of the ocean the ship
bound for America sails on alone with no sea gulls fluttering
about. And as the ship comes close to America, the American
sea gulls, who had been following some ship bound for France,
turn around and follow the ship that just came from France
back to their homeland.

It so happened that when the time came for the French
sea gulls to return to France a great storm came up!

Gogo and the other French sea gulls began to choose a ship that was sailing back to France.

But Gogo would not follow just any ship. He flew about sniffing at the ships trying to pick the one that might be serving the best dinner.

He sniffed at one ship . . . He smelled too much pepper in the stew cooking on that ship and he whirled away. Then he tried another ship and still another . . . None of them smelled as if they were having a very good dinner that evening.

Meanwhile the storm grew stormier and stormier. The waves rolled and tumbled over the whole surface of the ocean.

Aboard the good ship *Queen of France* they served (as they always did) an excellent dinner. The main dish was a gigantic omelet with mushrooms. It was followed by an elegant tossed salad and for dessert . . . delicious, tiny wild strawberries with great mounds of whipped cream!

The Chief Chef of the *Queen of France* always cooked a gigantic omelet of some sort during a storm . . because the rocking and the tossing of the ship on the stormy ocean helped mix the eggs for the gigantic omelet. His stormy weather omelets were always light and frothy. And his storm-tossed salad, too, was always a great success.

But not on this particular evening!

The ship bobbed and whirled and rolled so much that most of the passengers and most of the crew, including the captain, were seasick. No one on board the *Queen of France* wanted any dinner at all . . . except little Marianna!

She ate and enjoyed every scrap of her dinner and rushed out to the rolling deck to stand with the Chief Chef as he watched the leftovers thrown overboard.

Together they watched as the biggest, the most magnificent omelet the Chief Chef had ever cooked (so he said as he sadly leaned over the ship's rail), and about a ton and a half of tossed salad, and forty-four barrels of wild strawberries with whipped cream were thrown into the seething ocean!

This food was not leftovers! It was the complete dinner prepared by the excellent Chief Chef for 1,751 passengers aboard the *Queen of France!*

Well! When Gogo saw the large trays of golden omelet thrown off the *Queen of France,* he dropped the cold boiled potato he had picked up near another ship and flew as swift as a bullet to eat that delicious dinner. In an instant the other French gulls joined him. All the gulls greedily gobbled up the omelet and went on to the tossed salad and at last to the wild strawberries and whipped cream.

(It is a well-known scientific fact that sea gulls never become seasick. No matter how stormy the weather, they can always eat.)

The other sea gulls had some trouble getting a good share of the tiny wild strawberries and whipped cream because, as the globs of whipped cream hit the ocean they promptly mixed with the foam churned up by the stormy waters. Some sea gulls who swooped down for what looked like a sweet glob of cream, rose hastily because their beaks scooped up a nasty mouthful of salty sea foam instead.

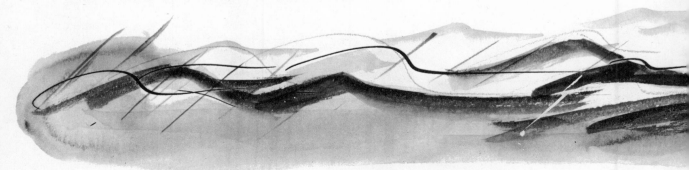

But not GOGO!

He found that by flying directly into the stream of wild strawberries and whipped cream as it was poured over the rails . . . with his mouth wide open . . . he did very well.

Soon all the other sea gulls, who never thought of flying into the strawberries and whipped cream with their mouths wide open, gave up. They flew off to follow the ships sailing back to France. But Gogo stayed on.

The Chief Chef of the *Queen of France* was cheered up a little as he watched the gulls gobble up the wonderful omelet and salad he had prepared. But when they flew away as the wild strawberries and whipped cream were poured over the side he was sad again.

"The stupid ones," he said to himself out loud. "They too know nothing of good food . . the most delicious dessert that ever . . ."

"No, no," shouted Marianna above the roar of the storm. "Look! . . . look at Gogo! . . . He is eating his dessert, too."

"Yes, you are right," cried the Chief Chef. "This is a wise one. He knows what is good and how to eat it . . . This gull is a great gourmet!"

(Gourmet is French and it means just that . . . one who knows good food and knows how to eat it.)

"Regard this brave sea gull!" bellowed the Chief Chef, to the men who had thrown the food overboard. "This sea gull is truly a great gourmet! Neither storm nor rain can keep him from eating good food when it is served."

All the men nodded and hastily carried the empty containers into the ship. It was raining very hard by this time.

"Good-by, Gogo, good-by," shouted Marianna just before she left the deck. Naturally, she thought Gogo was now going to fly back to France.

But Gogo did not fly back to France!

He found himself alone in the sky buffeted by the wind and pelted by the rain. There were no longer any other ships in sight and no other sea gulls . . . not a single one. He was afraid he might get lost if he tried to return home to France with no ship to guide him. So he continued to follow the *Queen of France* on her journey across the Atlantic Ocean.

The next morning the waters were calm. The Chief Chef arose very early. He had to again plan something very special for the 1,752 passengers aboard the *Queen of France* because, as always happened when the passengers had been seasick, they had no appetite the following morning. He racked his brain . . . what should he cook to tempt their appetites for breakfast?

How would it look if 1,751 thin, weak, underfed passengers were to walk down the gangplank when the *Queen of France* reached New York?

"I have it," he shouted as he banged the table with the palm of his hand. "I have it . . . Petites crêpes . . . tiny pancakes that my mother would serve me when I did not feel well . . . yes, tiny, delicate, tender, beautiful pancakes with currant jelly. No one can resist them."

Then in a very short time the Chief Chef had all his assistant cooks mixing great bowls of batter from the special secret recipe he had learned from his mother. And that morning hundreds . . . thousands . . . yes, almost a hundred thousand tiny pancakes (97,431 to be exact) dripping with currant jelly were served to the delighted 1,752 passengers aboard the *Queen of France*. Most of the passengers ate at least thirty pancakes. Some ate more.

Marianna alone ate forty-one pancakes before she left the table! It was true, as the Chief Chef had said, no one could resist these beautiful tiny pancakes.

Right after breakfast Marianna joined the Chief Chef as he leaned over the rail and watched the leftovers thrown overboard. The Chief Chef beamed! Not so much as a shred of pancake or one drop of currant jelly was thrown away! All that was tossed over the side of the *Queen of France* that morning were orange skins and old coffee grounds.

Marianna and all the assistant cooks gathered around the Chief Chef and congratulated him because not one of the 1,752 passengers had refused to eat his or her breakfast.

"It was nothing," said the Chief Chef modestly. "It was just something I learned at my mother's knee. But look there . . . there is one who has not been served!"

The Chief Chef pointed at one lone sea gull who whirled and swooped as he sampled the leftovers from that great ship, the *Queen of France*.

It was Gogo! He had nibbled on a bit of orange peel and whirled and swooped as he dropped it and picked up another bit. But there was nothing worth eating.

"It is the great gourmet!" cried the Chief Chef. "He has been faithful to us when all others refused our excellent dessert last night. Perhaps he is following us to America! How would it look if a faithful French sea gull following this great ship were to arrive in America hungry because of starvation?"

The Chief Chef turned to his assistant cooks and shouted:

"Go to the ship's big icebox and bring some good fresh raw fish and fine fresh raw vegetables . . such things as sea gulls love to eat. We shall reward this faithful sea gull Gogo for his loyalty to the *Queen of France.*"

As soon as the plates of raw fish and vegetables were brought out, the Chief Chef himself tossed the carefully chosen good fresh raw fish and vegetables to Gogo.

But Gogo tried a bit of raw fish and dropped it. And then he nibbled on a fresh red radish and gave that up, too. He no longer dove for the raw food that the Chief Chef threw over the side.

"What is this, my little one?" cried the Chief Chef. "You have lost your appetite? You are not hungry?"

Marianna tugged at the Chief Chef's apron.

"Yes, I think he *is* hungry," said Marianna. "But I think Gogo only loves good food . . . well-cooked! That's what makes him a special sea gull . . . I think he would love some of those delicious little pancakes . . ."

The Chief Chef slapped his forehead with his open hand.

"Of course! Yes, it must be true," shouted the Chief Chef. "Very well . . . to the kitchen. I shall cook for him as I would cook for only a great gourmet."

And in a few minutes the Chief Chef *himself* tossed a great portion of tiny delicious pancakes dripping with currant jelly over the side of the ship, one by one . . . while they were still hot! And grateful Gogo gobbled them up as fast as they were tossed.

For the next few days, just before the excellent meals were served on the *Queen of France,* the Chief Chef would wander through his kitchens and he would choose particularly fine portions of food to be set aside.

And after lunch (or dinner or breakfast) had been served to the 1,752 passengers, the Chief Chef himself would see that Gogo was served this delicious food he had put aside for him.

Gogo was very happy and grew quite fat in the next few days. And although the *Queen of France* was making a slow trip to America because she had been damaged in the storm, Gogo had some trouble keeping up with the ship.

And then one morning a great flock of American sea gulls who had been following a ship toward France whirled around and started back to America. They swooped down on the *Queen of France* just as the luncheon leftovers were being tossed overboard.

These American sea gulls were lean, hard and swift. Poor Gogo had not a chance when one of these swift-flying birds raced him for a fine morsel of food.

The Chief Chef tried again and again to toss special tidbits to Gogo. But even he could not ward off the eager American strangers. After a while the Chief Chef gave up trying to feed Gogo . . . he had so many other things to do.

But little Marianna saved her food so that she could feed Gogo. She ate almost nothing in the dining room and would gather food in her napkin. Then when she brought the food out on deck and tried to feed Gogo the strong American sea gulls would gobble the food right out of her napkin the moment she opened it up.

Poor fat Gogo got nothing!

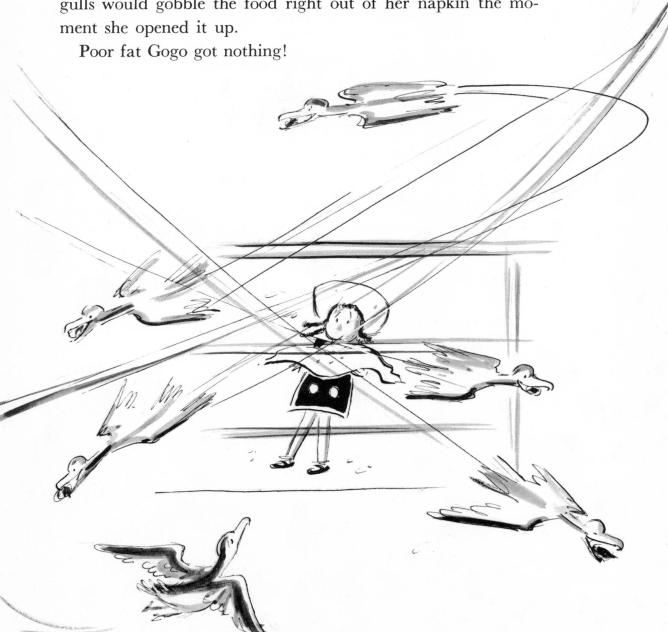

On the day that the *Queen of France* steamed into New York harbor, a heavy fog covered the ocean. Gogo, hungry and tired, was far behind the ship and the American sea gulls that followed it. And as the day wore on, he finally lost the ship and gulls altogether.

That evening Marianna said to her mother, "Mama, I am so worried about poor Gogo."

And her mother patted Marianna on the head and said, "Now don't you worry about that bird. I am quite sure he can take care of himself."

"But Mama," said Marianna, "will I ever see Gogo again?"

"Maybe . . and maybe not," said her mother. "But I am quite sure of one thing . . . you will hear about that bird again. Now go to sleep. We leave the ship early tomorrow."

Meanwhile out in the cold, damp night, poor, tired Gogo flew on alone. Now the fog had become so thick Gogo could not see beyond the length of his beak. Suddenly he bumped against something head on. Clunk!

He flew up, hoping to fly over the thing that he had bumped into. Up . . . up . . . up he flew! Was there no end to this huge obstacle?

At last Gogo came to the top of whatever it was he was trying to fly over. By this time he was so tired he could fly no farther. Gogo rested there and waited for the fog to lift, all through that dismal night.

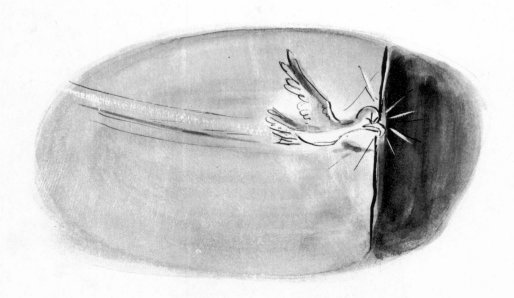

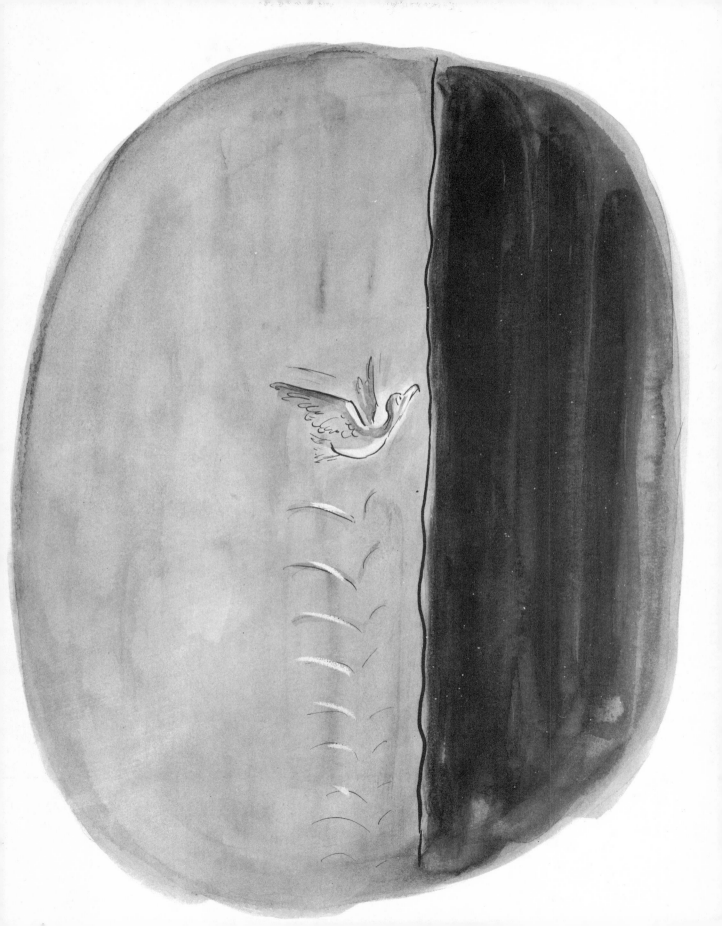

The next morning dawned bright and clear. What a sight met the eyes of Gogo, the French sea gull! For the first time he saw the great harbor of New York . . the biggest, busiest, richest harbor in the world!

He was sitting on (although naturally he did not know it) the topmost spike on the crown of the Statue of Liberty! That famous statue, as any schoolchild knows, looks proudly out to sea and welcomes travelers to the New York harbor. Gogo looked down at the thousands of ships going every which way in the harbor. They were all strangers to him.

After a while he flew down from his high perch to try to find the *Queen of France*. During his flight he followed an excursion boat all around the island of Manhattan. There were children on that boat who kept tossing out the last ends of some hot dogs and Bologna sandwiches they had eaten.

Gogo liked the hot dog ends. They were something like the tiny sausages the Chief Chef on the *Queen of France* sometimes served. But he did not care for the Bologna sandwiches at all . . . there was too much mustard on them.

For the next few days he spent all the daylight hours exploring the great New York harbor as he hunted for his favorite ship, the *Queen of France*. But Gogo could not find that great ship. She had been towed to a shipyard to have a propeller, damaged by the storm, repaired.

Now that Gogo had not eaten very well for a number of days he was not so fat. Again he became a strong, lean, swift-flying young sea gull. Every night he returned to the same perch on the great spikes on the crown of the Statue of Liberty. There he perched alone.

At last one morning, as Gogo flew down from his perch, he saw some very familiar bits of paper floating on the water at the foot of the Statue of Liberty. They were the little ruffles of paper which good chefs put around the end bones of broiled lamb chops. And these paper ruffles were not ordinary paper ruffles! They were larger and lacier than the ordinary ones. And each of them bore the stamp of a beautiful French flower! A fleur-de-lis!

Gogo recognized those ruffles at once! They were the special paper ruffles that the Chief Chef of the *Queen of France* always put on the thick crisp lamb chops he served his passengers!

There was a trail of ruffles leading right out to sea. Surely during the night the *Queen of France* must have passed that way!

Gogo took off at once along the trail of the *Queen of France*. He flew hard and swift all through that day. And at last, just as the sun was beginning to set, he saw a cloud of sea gulls fluttering over a great ship.

It *was* the *Queen of France,* followed by the American sea gulls! Gogo burned up the air around him as he sped toward his favorite ship. He arrived just in time to see the first bucket of leftovers tossed over the side. Dinner had been served and Gogo had arrived in the nick of time!

The Chief Chef had prepared a real American dish for the passengers. He always cooked an American dish on the first night out of New York harbor so that the passengers, who were mainly Americans traveling to Europe, would not be homesick.

For dinner that night he served "Haricot Blanc Boulanger à la Boston." That was a very long French title and the passengers did not know what it was even after some of them ate it.

It was really just Boston Baked Beans!

But the Chief Chef had given a few extra touches to this fine old American dish. He had spiced the beans with quite a bit of pepper and garlic and doused them with fine white wine vinegar. And he finished them off with a great sprinkling of mushrooms, truffles and broiled snails!

That evening there were a lot of leftovers for the gulls!

The Chief Chef leaned sadly on the rail as he watched the great portions of beans dumped overside. Even the American sea gulls were not happy with the Chief Chef's special American dish that evening.

But when Gogo threw himself joyfully into the stream of beans being poured overside, and ate with such gusto, the other sea gulls looked at the beans with more respect. And they ate them too.

"Regard! He has returned!" shouted the Chief Chef. "The great gourmet has returned . . . Vive la France!"

And all the assistant cooks shouted, "Vive la France!" with him.

It was not that Gogo really approved of the Chief Chef's beans. It was just that he was so happy to find his favorite ship again he would have eaten anything that was tossed overboard . . . even old Bologna sandwiches with too much mustard!

Naturally, Gogo followed his favorite ship, the *Queen of France,* all the way back to his native land. And on that voyage back to France, and from then on as long as he lived, Gogo ate better food than any other sea gull in the world because it was especially prepared for him by the great Chief Chef of the *Queen of France.*

And although Marianna never did see Gogo again, she heard about him. Because one day she got a letter . . . a letter with a photograph of Gogo in it, from the Chief Chef of the *Queen of France!* (They had exchanged addresses just before she left the ship.)

The Chief Chef wrote Marianna that Gogo had found the ship again, and he went on to say that he, the Chief Chef of the *Queen of France,* the greatest chef who sailed the seas, had made up a special dish in honor of Gogo, the special sea gull.

It was called "Petites Crêpes Suprême à la Gogo, le Gourmet."

That means "Gogo the Gourmet's supreme little pancakes." It was made up of beans, wild strawberries, whipped cream and broiled snails served on tiny pancakes!

(And strange to tell, it was delicious.)